Posie the Kitten in Pink

Sarah Phillips · Stuart Lynch

make
believe
ideas

Posie's the smallest kitten in town.

Her tail is smooth and her paws are round,

but her coat is covered in different patches

of colour and pattern – NOTHING matches!

"I'm a fright," moans Posie, "a terrible sight!

A mix and a mess of black, grey and white,

with splodges and stripes of ginger and brown,

a comical ear and a crazy frown!"

"Don't be depressed," says Midge the Mouse.
"Let's go for a stroll towards my house

and have some fun with the things we find
in the bits and bobs that are left behind."

The **friends** spy something **long** and **thin**,
peeking out of the **garbage bin.**

Is it a **bird?**

What could it **be?**

They **decide** to set the

creature

free!

They **push** and **shove**
and **drag** and **pull**
the **heavy** bin,
but it's too **full**.

At last it **starts** to
tip and **sway**.
Take care!
Keep out of the w.

The **pink** bird-animal is in a heap.

"Perhaps," says **Midge**, "it's **fast** asleep?"

"Maybe," adds **Posie**,

"we've got it **wrong**

and it's **no** animal

but a long, long . . ."

" . . . SCARF, soft, feathery and pink!

The colour suits don't you think?

Wow! Now Posie glitters and glows,
and sparkles from her head to her toes.

Midge stares and can't believe his eyes.
He hops from foot to foot and cries:

"The Kitten in Pink, that's what you are,
a dazzling, beautiful superstar!
All cats will stop and gaze at you
and follow what you say and do!"

The friends run through the park and see
Little Lil by the big oak tree.

"I've lost my rope; I'm all alone.
It's no fun playing on your own!"

FRED'S
FISH

Posie suggests,
"Let's use my scarf
to help Lil skip
and make her laugh!"

The feathers tickle and Little Lil giggles;
as she skips, she wiggles and wriggles.

They hear a cry as Granny Cat slips
and scatters wool as she trips.
Three naughty kitties want some fun –
they grab the balls and start to run.

The kitties stare and are filled with shame.

They bring the wool, and feeling sad,

say sorry to Granny for being bad.

Suddenly up run two big cats,
carrying black sacks on their backs.

Now Posie thinks and moves at speed,
Most keen to help a cat in need.

One thief is caught with
a pink lasso,

a **woollen** web
catches number **two**.

"To thank you," Bob says, "please do take your pick of any of my cakes."

As **they** start eating cakes and pies,
big, black **rain clouds** fill the **skies**.

Rain washes all the glitter away.
Posie shone pink for one short day,
but she's happy now and will worry less
that her mixed-up coat is a funny mess.

The **important** thing is what **you** do,
not whether **your** coat is **pink** or **blue**.
Helping those who are **stuck** or **sad**
makes them **happy** and leaves you **glad!**